This book is dedicated to
Liz and Gerry, Candy, Bill,
Megan, Steve, and Darrell
Love, Todd

First Edition

Library of Congress Cataloging-in-Publication Data
Parr, Todd.
  Do's and don'ts / Todd Parr. — 1st ed.
     p.   cm.
  Summary: In illustrations and brief text, presents twelve rules to live by,
accompanied by silly alternatives, such as "Do help keep the house
clean" and "Don't vacuum up the cat."
  ISBN 0-316-69213-1
  [1. Conduct of life — Fiction. 2. Behavior — Fiction.] I. Title.
PZ7.P2447Do 1999
[E] — dc21   98-3284

10 9 8 7 6 5 4 3

TWP

Printed in Singapore

Do's AND Don'ts

TODD PARR

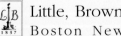

Little, Brown and Company
Boston New York London

DO

Change your socks every day

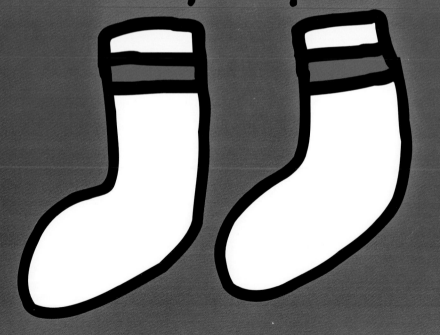

Don't

make anyone smell them

Do

Have Lunch with a monkey

Don't

Eat his bananas

Do

Help keep the House clean

Don't

Vacuum up the CAT

DO

smile at people

Stick your tongue
out at them

Eat all the Food on Your Plate

Don't

put it in your Hair

DO

Give the Dog a bath

Don't

Take one with him

wear clean underwear

Don't

wear it on your head

DO

Eat cookies and milk before you go to bed

MILK

Don't

Get a Tummy ache

DO

wear your Dad's Pajamas

Don't

wear them to school

HA HA HA HA

DO

Give kisses to everyone you love

Don't

kiss a cootie Bug

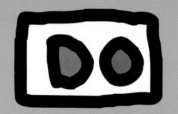

DO

Brush your teeth after Every meal

Brush with Peanut Butter

Butter

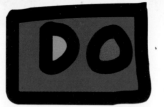

DO

Read a book at Bedtime

Don't

Stay up all night!